To Jack

Other Baby Bear books to share:

Is It Christmas?

Hold Tight!

The Big Baby Bear Book

Again!

Walking Round the Garden

Number One, Tickle Your Tum

The Bear Went Over the Mountain

Oh Where, Oh Where?

Clap Your Hands

I'm Coming to Get You!

BABY BEAR'S CHRISTMAS KISS
A Bodley Head Book 0 370 32686 5

First published in Great Britain in 2004 by The Bodley Head,
an imprint of Random House Children's Books

1 3 5 7 9 10 8 6 4 2

RANDOM HOUSE CHILDREN'S BOOKS
61–63 Uxbridge Road, London W5 5SA
A division of The Random House Group Ltd
RANDOM HOUSE AUSTRALIA (PTY) LTD
20 Alfred Street, Milsons Point, Sydney,
New South Wales 2061, Australia
RANDOM HOUSE NEW ZEALAND LTD
18 Poland Road, Glenfield, Auckland 10, New Zealand
RANDOM HOUSE (PTY) LTD
Endulini, 5A Jubilee Road, Parktown 2193, South Africa

THE RANDOM HOUSE GROUP Limited Reg. No. 954009
www.kidsatrandomhouse.co.uk

A CIP catalogue record for this book is available from the British Library.

Printed and bound in Singapore

Baby Bear's Christmas Kiss

JOHN PRATER

THE BODLEY HEAD
LONDON

It was Christmas Day!
The whole family were visiting Baby Bear and
Grandbear. That's Granny Bear, Uncle Bear,
Auntie Bear and four Cousin Bears.
The grown-ups warmed up by the fire,
while the little ones put their presents
under the tree. But they didn't seem
to be able to leave them alone.

Every present was shaken . . .

. . . prodded

. . . and sniffed.

Grandbear had an idea.
"You can open just one
present each, now!"

All the cousins ripped open their presents.

"Wow!" said Baby Bear. "What is it?"
"It's a toboggan," said Grandbear.
"What's a 'boggan?"
asked Baby Bear.
"I'll show you,"
said Uncle Bear.
"Come outside with me."

"Up the hill
we go!"
said Uncle Bear.

"Now watch closely,"
said Uncle Bear.
"First, you . . ."

"Hey!" cried Uncle Bear. "Wait! . . ."

Faster and *faster*
    went Uncle Bear . . .

. . . until he met up with a snowbear!

"That was really funny," said Baby Bear.
"Can we have a go, now?"

Up the hill
they went again . . .

. . . and down

they came!

Again and again until Uncle Bear said . . . .

"Oooh, I can smell yummy cooking.
It's time to go inside."

Grandbear met them at the door.
"Hello, snowbears! You're just
in time for Christmas dinner."

What a feast!

After dinner, the grown-ups were so
full they could hardly move.
The little ones played hide-and-seek.

It didn't take Baby Bear long to find Big Cousin Bear hiding under the tree. "This is my present to Mum and Dad," said Big Cousin Bear. "What are you giving Grandbear?"

"I haven't got a present for Grandbear!" said Baby Bear. "Never mind," said Big Cousin Bear. "It's your turn to hide now!"

While the others covered their eyes, and counted to ten, Baby Bear crept out of the room, through the kitchen, and into the garden.

But Baby Bear wasn't hiding. Baby Bear was going to find a present for Grandbear.

Grandbear likes snow, thought Baby Bear.
And stars. Something glistened and caught
Baby Bear's eye . . .

Baby Bear looked closer.
"Snowberries!"
said Baby Bear.
"All twinkly like
the star on the
Christmas
tree!"

Baby Bear picked
some berries, then
started to make
something out
of snow.

When it was
finished,
Baby Bear
hurried
back inside.

"Found you!"
called Cousin Bear.
"Come on, we're opening
the presents now."

Everyone was very excited!

"Happy Christmas, Grandbear!" said Baby Bear. "I brought you a snowberry snowbear!"

"Mistletoe!" said Grandbear. "That deserves a special Christmas kiss! I'll put your lovely present somewhere where it won't melt."

All the grown-ups asked

if they could have a

Christmas kiss too.

The little ones weren't too sure, though.